THE MAD MAGE'S ACADEMY

HALT, ADVENTURER, AND READ THESE WORDS BEFORE YOU PROCEED!

You are about to embark on a journey. To where, only you could possibly say. It is not a journey like any you have been on before, where you start at page one and continue on a straight course until you reach the end. Instead, you will be presented with many choices along the way. Each time you are faced with one such choice, make your decision from the options given and then follow the directions to continue your adventure. Once your quest has come to an end, either favorably or, as I'm afraid in some instances it is foretold to, gruesomely, return to the beginning or the last choice and try again.

This is not a journey for those who prefer to sit back and let others make the tricky decisions. This is a journey for a leader, a true hero. One who is not afraid to risk perilous traps, face all-powerful wizards, or steal well-protected artifacts. If this doesn't sound like you, turn back now and forget you ever came this way. But if this whiff of adventure has whet your appetite, then forward with you, my friend. And good luck!

CANDLEWICK
ENTERTAINMENT

DUNGEONS & DRAGONS

ENDLESS QUEST®

THE MAD MAGE'S ACADEMY

MATT FORBECK

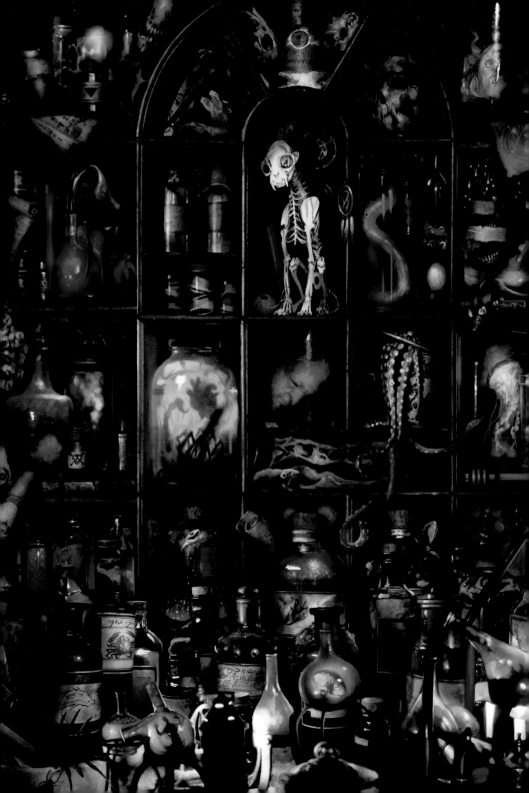

Y ou're an idiot.

Well, you're a great thief — the kind of swashbuckling rogue bards might someday sing epic ballads about — but recent evidence points to the fact that you may not be as sharp as even the knife in your belt.

Fact #1: You agreed to steal something from the Mad Mage, Halaster, one of the most dangerous wizards ever to darken the Sword Coast. Most thieves would have turned down the gig at the first mention of Halaster's name, but you didn't hesitate to accept your mission for even a second.

Fact #2: The thing you agreed to steal was Halaster's spell book. As powerful as the Mad Mage is, the theory goes, his spell book must be crammed to bursting with pages filled with notations and the secrets behind his most amazing spells.

Fact #3: According to the person who hired you to steal that spell book, it's safely hidden away in Dweomercore, an academy the Mad Mage set up so he could train the next generation of evil wizards to work for him.

Fact #4: The Mad Mage's academy is located on the ninth level of the massive dungeon known as Undermountain, which ripples through Mount Waterdeep, all the way from the magical metropolis of Waterdeep that sits atop it down to the roots of the mountain itself.

That's enough to convict you of being foolish for sure, if not outright stupid.

Still, you took the job. Because you think you might be able to pull it off. And if you do, you'll make yourself a legend throughout Waterdeep and beyond.

You came up with a plan so crazy it might just work. You decided to sneak your way into Dweomercore by posing as a wizard who's interested in studying at Halaster's academy. Once you get through the door, you hope to find the spell book, snatch it, and run off with it before anyone's any the wiser. With luck, you'll be back in Waterdeep, rolling in gold and glory, before the Mad Mage even knows his favorite spell book has gone missing.

So far, so good. You started at a Waterdeep inn called the Yawning Portal for the giant well in its basement that leads straight into Undermountain. From there, you worked your way down to the legendary dungeon's ninth level, doing your best to avoid any other sorts of entanglements, no matter how tempting they might have been. And now you find yourself standing outside the entrance to the Mad Mage's academy.

You walk down the hallway until it opens into a large room with a high arched ceiling covered from one end to the other with bright mosaics. You squint up at images of wand-wielding wizards engaged in stunning magical duels.

A withered, disembodied hand—severed long ago from its owner and now floating before you in midair—points at you as you enter the room and motions for you to stop. Not wanting to see what the hand might be able to do to you, you comply.

A moment later, a man with a long mane of white hair and an even longer and bushier white beard sweeps into the room.

"I'm Halaster Blackcloak, master of Dweomercore," he says. "Welcome to my academy. What business might you have here?"

You point up at the hand still floating in the middle of the room. "What's the story behind that?"

Halaster chuckles to himself. "That belonged to a wizard named Manshoon. He thought he was a much better duelist than it turned out was true. Now, answer my question. Why are you here?"

"Isn't it obvious?" you say with as much panache as you can muster. "I'm a young wizard-in-training, and I'd like to apply to study here at your academy."

The mage narrows his eyes at you, madness dancing in his pupils. "You don't look much like a wizard—whatever that means. Are you absolutely sure about that?"

Charge into the school. Turn to page 6 . . .
Attack Halaster! Turn to page 9 . . .
Apply to the school. Turn to page 17 . . .

I'm sorry," you say with a frown. "I'm not comfortable wandering around Wormriddle's quarters unannounced."

Medley pokes her head back into the room—but just her head, so it looks like it's floating in midair out of the smoke. "You already came this far. You didn't seem that concerned about it when you barged into her main hall," she says.

"Did I do something wrong by that? Spite led me here and told me to go in."

She gives you a suspicious glare. "Do you always do what people you've just met tell you to do?"

You peer into the smoke behind Medley's floating head. "Where did you say Wormriddle is again?"

"I didn't." She gives you a wicked smile. Then her entire head changes, becoming much larger, older, and bluer.

When her transformation is complete, she steps forward out of the smoke, revealing herself to be a night hag. You immediately realize that you've been talking to Wormriddle the entire time.

"I'm so sorry," you tell her as you back away. "I didn't mean to bother you."

"Don't lie to me," she says with a vicious cackle. Her voice has echoes of Medley's, but it's much lower and meaner. Murderous even. "That's exactly what you came here for—or at least why Spite sent you here. Don't try to deny it!"

You give her a helpless shrug. There's really nothing you could say that might placate her.

"Halaster may like to let the applicants wander about the place, but I've warned him about this. You're lucky I don't skin you alive and make use of your best parts in my golem laboratory," says Wormriddle.

You don't like the way this is going and cast an eye around for a way out. With all the smoke filling the room, you suspect that you could easily make a run for it.

"I can see what you're thinking," the hag croons. "And I can assure you that it'll do you no good. You already made a big mistake by coming here uninvited. Don't be so stupid as to make another."

The tone of her voice suggests that it doesn't really matter what you do now; you're done for. Logic says why not try for the door anyway? So you do. You drop to the floor where the smoke is at its thickest and scuttle for the exit as fast as you can. But you're not quick enough. A few mumbled words from Wormriddle, and your body goes stiff and lifts above the cover of the smoke. She grins down at you, cackling maniacally, and you know you're not getting out of here alive.

THE END

Applying to study at the school seems like a lot of work, and honestly, you just can't be bothered with that right now. This is supposed to be a burglary, after all, not a new career.

It would be simplest just to attack Halaster and take the spell book from him, but the way that floating hand hovers over his shoulder, you figure he's too smart to let you have any actual chance of hurting him. You're better off dashing past him, finding the spell book, and doing a smash-and-grab on it instead.

So that's what you do. Halaster entered the room by a stout wooden door to the east, and he didn't bother to close it behind him. There are other ways out of the room, but that seems like your best bet. Without another word, you charge straight past Halaster and race through it.

Halaster flinches as you pass him, perhaps thinking you were going to attack him. When he sees that you're running straight into the academy instead, though, he just throws back his head and laughs.

"I've rarely seen someone so eager to join our ranks!" he calls after you. "But if you think you're fooling anyone, my speedy thief, you should quit fooling yourself."

You wince at the fact that the wizard saw through you so quickly, but you realize you shouldn't be surprised. It's hard to fool anyone that smart—which is exactly why you decided to charge into this place, right?

You reach an intersection just beyond the door. The well-lit hallway continues straight on to the east, and you can see various passageways on either side. A light blazes in a distant room at the far end.

To the south, the passageway seems to open up for a moment before continuing. You think you see a statue of some sort in a room at the end of the hall, but it's hard to tell what it might be from here.

Turn south. Turn to page 12 . . .
Continue east. Turn to page 14 . . .

As Halaster awaits your reply, you suddenly rethink your whole plan. Sure, it might have seemed like a good idea to worm your way into the academy by lying about your plans to study here, but a mage like Halaster is sure to see through you sooner or later, right?

Better if you just drop all the pretenses right now and take your best shot at the man. At least it's cleaner that way. If you're going to live or die here, why bother with all the lying and hiding and scuttling about? Better to find out sooner rather than later what your fate might be.

Or so you think.

You draw your sword, fast as a flash, and put the blade to Halaster's throat. Before the mage can react, you have him at your mercy. All it would take is a flick of your wrist, and you'd have him bleeding to death on the floor.

"I'm here for your spell book," you tell the surprised man. "Take me straight to it, and you might yet survive this."

Halaster stares at you, his eyes wide in shock, and for a moment you think this new, faster plan of yours might go well. Then the man starts laughing.

What are you supposed to make of this? He doesn't seem scared at all. When he gives you a pitiful shake of his head, you realize you're the one in deep trouble.

Still, you press the blade to his throat, just hard enough to draw a crimson line of blood across it. The shallow cut doesn't stop the man from laughing.

"I'd rather not kill you, but I won't hesitate if I have to," you say.

"You think you're the first fool to come here and try to rob Halaster?" the man says. "You're not even the first one this week!"

Unnerved, you grab the man by the hair on the back of his head and shove your blade into his throat. You expect him to fall over and die in your arms, but your sword doesn't sink into his flesh. It just slides off it as if his skin were made of impervious armor.

Halaster disappears then, right before your eyes. You realize that you're no longer holding the head of a man but that of a red-furred fox. You look down and see that his exposed hands and feet are now fur-covered paws, and a long, bushy tail snakes out of the rear of his robes.

"What in all the gods' names?" you say as you leap backward from the creature.

"I'm not even Halaster," the monster says through rows of vicious teeth. "He's too busy to be bothered running a school like this. I'm a demon disguised as him."

You're terrified, but you've gone too far to turn back now.

"I don't suppose we could come to some sort of deal?"

The fox-faced demon laughs even harder than before. "There's nothing you could offer me that could possibly make me betray the real Halaster. In fact, let me make a suggestion for you. . . ."

With that, he pulls something oily from a pocket in his wizardly robes and waves it in your direction as he chants a few words in a language that hurts your ears. Then the world begins to seem fuzzier and simpler than you ever remember. Through the cloud that settles over your brain, you hear the demon speak.

"There are many monsters in this land less fortunate than an adventurer like you. Go as far into the Undermountain as you can and give one of them your sword. For keeps."

You want to argue with the fox-man—to tell him that his suggestion seems unwise—but you can't muster the strength of will. Instead, you find yourself turning around and trudging away. As you trundle into the darkness, echoes of the demon's laughter chase you down the passageway, and you wonder if that'll be the last thing you hear.

The moment you leave the academy behind, though, you realize you don't know how to get deeper into Undermountain from here. Your only option is to head toward Waterdeep. On your way back upward, you spy a pack of goblins. You sneak up and throw your sword at them.

"Keep it!" you shout at the startled monsters as you sprint away at top speed . . . before one of them has the idea to plant the blade in your back.

THE END

You figure that heading toward a statue is probably a better bet than charging into a well-lit room that might be packed with people. As you sprint to the south, hoping to outrun whatever sorts of spells Halaster might hurl after you, you pass a set of eight portraits, each depicting a staff-wielding wizard representing one of the eight different schools of magic.

You know there are eight schools of magic, but you couldn't rattle them off in a list, not even with a wand to your head. That's part of why you chose to ditch the whole "pretend to be a wizard" scheme. You probably wouldn't have gotten very far with it anyhow.

You begin to rethink your decision, though, when you realize that the statue you're heading toward is that of a snake-haired woman: a medusa!

At least you hope it's a statue. The figure is holding a longbow with an arrow notched against its string, but it hasn't moved a muscle the whole time you've been looking at it.

The irony of a creature that can turn victims to stone with a glance being carved out of stone isn't lost on you. You just hope its gaze doesn't work. . . .

Turn to page 15 . . .

12

You can't let this tiefling slow you down. You draw your rapier and stab at her.

The young wizard leaps behind her desk, putting it between you and her. As she goes, she fishes a bit of glass from her pocket and crushes it on the back of the desk. She spits out a word you can't understand, but the moment it leaves her lips, a cloud of daggers surrounds you, the blades swirling and spinning.

You do your best to parry as many of them as you can, but the ones you miss stab and slash at you time and again. One of them catches you in the throat, and you go down, clutching at the wound.

You roll onto your back, unable even to gasp for help. From the look on the tiefling's face, she wouldn't have given it to you anyhow.

"I'll have to have a talk with Halaster about the kinds of visitors he allows in the school," she says with a disappointed grimace as the darkness takes you. "We can't just have people coming in to stab us like this."

THE END

Better to race toward an empty room rather than toward one with someone — or something — standing in it, or so you hope. You charge straight down the hallway, blasting past several other doors and passages. Once you reach the room at the end of the hall, though, you find that it isn't as empty as you had hoped.

To the northeast, there's a door with a plaque on it that reads "Headmaster's Office — Knock Please." But that's not all.

A young woman sitting at a desk in the room leaps to her feet as you enter, her robes whirling about her. She has purplish skin, red eyes, and sharp horns that arc backward from the center of her forehead to wrap around her long blue hair. You recognize her as a tiefling, a humanoid people descended from otherworldly demons.

The woman has been reading a scorched spell book — probably not the one you're searching for, by the looks of it, as it's rather new and thin.

"Who are you, and what are you doing here?" she asks, baring her sharp, pointed teeth.

Those are fair questions, you realize. Given the circumstances, there are really only two ways to answer them.

Ask her for help. Turn to page 90...
Attack her! Turn to page 13...

Normally, you might haul up short rather than charging straight toward a statue of a medusa, but the fact that Halaster is somewhere behind you spurs you forward. The closer you get, the surer you become that the figure before you is a statue.

Then you feel something . . . odd. You realize you've somehow triggered a magical trap, and you wish that you'd bothered to study some actual magic after all.

The statue standing before you springs to life. At least it's still just a statue, you tell yourself. If it had transformed into an actual medusa, you'd probably be a statue already yourself.

Instead of petrifying you with its gaze, the medusa aims its bow at you and lets the arrow in it fly. You try to throw yourself to the side, but the arrow strikes you in the arm.

"Ahhh!" you scream in pain. You've been shot before, and this hurts much worse than it should. You pull the arrow from the wound, and you see that it's dripping with a greenish-black fluid—poison! That's when you realize you're in real trouble.

You feel the need to sit down, and the hallway around you begins to fade to black. You think maybe the statue is laughing at you, but just before you expire, you see that the voice is that of Halaster—who looms and cackles over you—instead.

THE END

O f course I'm sure!" you say. "What young wizard wouldn't want to study under the legendary Halaster Blackcloak? I consider it an honor that you didn't vaporize me the moment I crossed the threshold to your school."

Halaster strokes his beard, amused. "The day is still young."

You laugh off the implied threat and hope you don't sound as nervous as you are. "So, what do I need to do to get started?" you ask. "Cast a spell? Kill a monster? Go on a quest?"

"We don't bother with such things here," Halaster says. "We simply administer a test to see if you're good material for our academy."

You nod, hoping that you can somehow skip that part, as you don't know how well you're going to be able to fake being an actual wizard. If you're going to bluff your way through this, though, you can't show an instant's hesitation.

"When do we get started?" you ask.

Halaster waves, and the hand floating above him retreats to a distant corner of the room.

"I'm sure you've had a long journey and would like to freshen up. We want to make sure you're rested and sharp before we administer the exam. You wouldn't believe how many people fail after insisting that they're absolutely fine and ready to start right away. Do yourself a favor and accept our hospitality. It's freely offered and given with no strings attached."

The wizard's tone tells you he won't allow you to say

no, despite how much you'd rather not get settled in. If you unpack your things, then you'll have to gather them up again before you leave — or just abandon them, which you'd rather not do. Despite that, you give him a grateful nod and gesture for him to lead the way into the school.

"If you insist," you say.

Halaster snorts and then turns to usher you back through the door via which he entered. You emerge into a long hallway that leads straight off to the east. Another hallway spurs off to the south, but he leads you past that to take the next turn to the right, into another long hallway.

This one is lined with three doors on either side and comes to a dead end. Halaster takes you halfway down the hall and opens the door on the right, then motions for you to enter the small room beyond.

"This hall features one of our two student dormitories," he tells you. "Conveniently, this room is empty at the moment, so you can rest here. In fact, if you make it into the school, this room will be yours. Feel free to take as long as you like."

"I'm sure I'll be ready to go soon," you say as you slide past Halaster and into the room.

It's a decent size and contains a bed, dresser, and chest, along with a desk and chair. Everything you'd need for your studies, if you happened to be an actual wizard.

An ever-burning torch flickers above the desk, and a row of five tubes lines the wall nearest the door. Halaster notices you examining them.

"Those are part of our pneumatic tube messaging system. You can put notes in the proper tubes, and air elementals carry them where they're needed. The one labeled 'Headmaster's Office' goes right to me. When you're ready to get started, just let me know."

"Thank you for your hospitality," you say as you stifle a fake yawn. "I suppose the trip here really has tired me out."

Halaster laughs. "You're wise to take my advice," he says before bustling from the room and closing the door behind him.

You hustle over to the thick door and put your ear to it so you can listen to him leave. When you're confident that he's gone, you walk over to the bed and sit on it for a moment to contemplate your options.

Halaster wasn't wrong—you are tired—but you have a job to do. The question is, how should you do it? Should you take a nap and wait for him to return to ask after you? Or should you take advantage of the fact that Halaster doesn't seem to be watching you right now, so you can wander around the academy without worrying about him looking over your shoulder?

You stare at the door for a moment as you make up your mind.

Wander around. Turn to page 26 . . .
Wait. Turn to page 28 . . .

M y name's Nylas Jowd," the Red Wizard says. "And I have a proposition for you."

You step back and gesture for the man to enter the room so you can speak privately, but he holds up a hand to refuse the kindness.

"We can surmise that you want to attend the academy?"

"That's a fair assumption," you grant with a nod.

"Unfortunately, the classes are full at the moment," Nylas says with a scowl. "Full of horrible people. People who shouldn't be here at all."

"What do you mean?"

Nylas glances around before leaning forward and speaking in a conspiratorial whisper. "Most of the students aren't even, well . . ." He looks at you and realizes you might not sympathize with what he's about to say. "The point is that the only way for you to gain admittance to the school would be for at least one of them to disappear. I can help you make that happen."

You don't want to get involved in such drama, but if it helps you to find the spell book you're after, you'll give it a shot.

"I'm listening," you encourage.

"There are two girls here: twins. Tieflings— half-demonic things. They don't even want to be here. Get rid of them, and a spot should open up for you."

Play along with the plot . . . for now. Turn to page 31 . . .
Refuse to help. Turn to page 35 . . .
Attack Nylas. Turn to page 36 . . .

I suppose I have to agree with that," you say.

It's best for the academy. Cephalossk stares at you with his unblinking black eyes, and you wonder if he's thinking about how your brain might taste.

You clear your throat. "So, why did you bring me here?"

The mind flayer closes the door to the room, and the place suddenly seems a lot smaller. You notice the stench now. It smells like an underground sea.

I need your help, and you need mine.

"How do you mean?" you ask, suspicious.

I have read your mind. You're here to steal Halaster's spell book. I can help you with that.

You glance at the door, wondering if you should make a break for it. "I don't know what you're talking about."

Deny it out loud. Smart. But we both know the truth.

Exasperated at having been found out so soon, you decide to be direct.

"What do you want?"

There's another who wishes to enroll at the school. His name's Spite Harrowdale, and he can't be allowed to remain here.

"Why don't you take care of that yourself?"

Spite has a bodyguard with him at all times. A half-ogre brute named Dumara. She's incredibly strong and wary of me to the point where I can't get past her without causing a scene. Worse, both of their minds have proven impervious to my attempts to probe them, and if I use my magic against them, it'll be obvious who took him out. And that I can't afford to have known.

"So why me?"

You are a newcomer—a stranger—so Spite and Dumara won't be as wary of you. They'll let you in closer. And anyway, I know Halaster, and by eliminating another student, you'll rise in his esteem and increase your chances of admittance to the school.

"You realize I don't actually want to attend classes here, right?"

The mind flayer chortles, sending his facial tentacles quaking. *Of course! I forgot that you're sure to leave as soon as you get what you're after. Even better! If you help me, I'll show you where Halaster keeps his spell book and then assist you in your escape.*

Refuse. Turn to page 33 . . .
Play along for now. Turn to page 40 . . .

Y ou turn and close the door behind you.

"Look," you say, attempting to step around the half-ogre who's cautiously moved to stand between you and the boy. "I have reason to believe your life is in danger. You need to leave this place."

The boy looks at you with alarm, but whatever he's feeling is rivaled by the shock that runs through you as Dumara starts to shudder and transform before your eyes. She grows larger and bluer, grunting in pain at the transformation. Her bared teeth have turned to razor-sharp points, and black claws the size of a bear's spring from her fingertips. She can be only one thing: an oni.

"Who are you? Who sent you?" she roars, taking a step toward you.

You retreat shakily until you stand with your back pressed against the door and reach for the handle.

"Wait!" you cry in desperation. "I came in here to warn you. That mind flayer down the hall? Cephalossk, is that his name? He wants you gone, and he's willing to kill you to get the job done."

The oni stops in her advance and considers you.

Turn to page 55...

You can't just sit around in this room waiting for Halaster to come fetch you. The longer you wait, the better chance someone has of uncovering you as a magic-less fraud.

You listen again to see if there's anyone moving in the hallway outside. Believing yourself to be alone, you open the door and are shocked to find a squid-faced human standing there, stock-still. Only its tentacles move, silently writhing at the bottom of its cephalopod face, right where its mouth should be.

I am the mind flayer Cephalossk, a voice that isn't your own says in your head. *I'm a student here at Dweomercore.*

It takes you but a moment to recover from your surprise. You give the tall, pale-skinned creature a shallow bow in response. "Good to meet you. I'm applying —"

Your purpose here is self-evident. The mind flayer glances in both directions. *Accompany me to my quarters so that we might speak in private.*

It doesn't seem worth it to point out that Cephalossk is speaking in a way that's impossible to overhear—or so you think. Instead, you follow the creature across the hallway to his own room.

The room is a mirror image of your own, although it's clearly more lived in. There's a bed in one corner that has no pillow, and an overflowing desk has been jammed against the other wall. The walls are damp with moisture, as slick as Cephalossk's skin. And they're lined with shelves of books, scrolls, and jars filled with a thick, translucent liquid, in some of which float perfectly preserved brains.

Those are for me. Cephalossk points at the brains. *Everyone asks about them.*

"Why are you studying them?" you ask, curious.

The mind flayer's facial tentacles quiver with silent laughter. *Oh, I don't study them. I eat them.*

You do your best to suppress your revulsion at that mental image, but you're sure you fail badly. "They permit that here?"

They prefer me eating these preserved brains to dining on fresh ones, I'm sure.

Turn to page 22...

You decide that Halaster was right. You've had a long-enough day. Reaching the ninth level of Undermountain was a tremendous task all by itself, and you're beat.

On top of that, it's not worth pushing your luck by exploring the academy on your own. Halaster might have a guard posted somewhere outside your room—or maybe even some kind of magical monitor—and you don't need to let him know that you're not who you seem to be.

At least not yet. You'll have other chances to look around, you tell yourself. All in good time.

You take your boots off and lie down on the bed. It's almost as comfortable as the rocky shelf you had to sleep on last night, but it'll do. After all, you're only going to shut your eyes for a few moments, right?

It turns out you're a lot more tired than you think. . . .

You have no idea how much later it is when you awaken to a gentle knock on the door.

"Just a moment," you say as you shove your feet back into your boots.

Grumbling silently to yourself, you scurry over to the door and throw it open. You fully expect Halaster to be standing there, ready to escort you away to take the entrance exam. Instead, you find a shaven-headed man dressed in a long red robe, staring at you with dark, sunken eyes.

While you've never met one of the Red Wizards before, you've heard all sorts of horrible stories about both them and the dangerous land of Thay from which they hail. The people of Thay live under the rule of a powerful group of wizards overseen by the evil necromancer Szass Tam. It only makes sense that one of them might wind up here to study under the Mad Mage.

The man regards you with an unforgiving stare, sizing you up as if you were nothing more to him than cattle.

"Can I help you?" you ask.

He purses his lips and nods. "That really is the question, isn't it?"

Turn to page 21 . . .

You haul Nylas's unconscious form into your room and start trying to stuff him under the bed. With luck, he won't wake up until long after you're gone, or so you hope.

It's not quite as easy as you'd like, though, and soon there's another knock at the door. You leap to your feet to answer it, hoping to keep whoever it is from entering. Before you can even reach the door, though, Halaster barges in.

You freeze for a moment, unsure what to do. Remembering the cosh you put back into your pocket, you feel around for it.

Halaster peers around you and spots Nylas's feet barely sticking out from under the bed. "Ooh!"

Backing away, you let the wizard push past you. Before you can attack, Halaster spins about and shakes your hand.

"Well done, young wizard!" he says with delight. "Well done!"

You goggle at him, confused.

He smiles at you. "You passed the test!"

"What?"

"The entrance exam. It's to see how you work with other students. To see if you're hard-edged enough to handle it here. You passed!"

You return the handshake, relieved and still a little confused. "Thanks."

"Allow me personally to offer you a coveted position at the Mad Mage's academy," he says. "Congratulations!"

Decline. Turn to page 50...
Accept. Turn to page 54...

That sounds like a fine plan," you say to Nylas. "But what's in it for you?"

Nylas smiles, impressed by your suspicions. "Those two tieflings have been a thorn in my side ever since they arrived. If you take them out, you'll be making this a much pleasanter place for me to study."

"And if I fail?"

Nylas shrugs. "Then I pin your demise on them and try to get them expelled for that."

"So it works out for you either way. But it might go poorly for me."

"That's the chance you took when you came down here to apply to the academy. You should be happy that I decided to take you under my wing."

The man turns and walks down the hallway, back the way you originally came. Following him, you come to a T junction at which he leads you to the right and escorts you toward a well-lit room at the end of the hall. As you creep closer, you see a young tiefling—a person of demonic descent—hunched over a desk, copying lines from a book.

Turn to page 34 . . .

You frown at the mind flayer, unsure as to what he's actually asking you to do here.

"I suppose you'd eat his brains after I take him down?"

It would be a waste to let a perfectly good brain just rot away.

You shudder in revulsion. "Forget it. I'll do what I have to on my own."

I'm delighted to hear that.

You freeze. "Why would that make you happy?"

I was hoping you'd help me, but if you find that impossible, then you're of no use to me in that way.

"Fine," you say as you move toward the door. "Then I'll be going."

Cephalossk blocks you.

There's another way in which you can be of use to me. A very delicious way.

You reach for your sword, but before you can draw it, the mind flayer's face darts forward, and his tentacles wrap themselves around your head.

You try to scream, but one of the tentacles snakes around your throat, cutting off your cry. Others hold you so tight you can't pull yourself free. You try to reach for your sword, but Cephalossk shouts into your brain, *BE STILL.*

And so you are. Right up until the end.

THE END

Nylas gives you a wink. "I'll leave you to your work," he whispers. Then he walks away.

You creep up behind the tiefling, who doesn't appear to notice you at all. All those years working as a thief in Waterdeep serve you well when it comes to padding silently across a floor.

It would be simple to just slip the point of your blade between the young wizard's ribs. She'd be dead in an instant. But needless killing has never really been your style, and frankly, you'd rather avoid it if you can.

After all, what if Nylas is setting you up to fail? If you kill the tiefling, will Halaster hold that against you? Might he not kick you out of the academy?

As you hesitate, the tiefling puts down her writing quill and squirms in her chair, restless.

"Well?" she says aloud. "Are you going to try to kill me or not?"

Maybe you're not quite as quiet as you think.

"How long have you known I was here?"

"You're actually a pretty good sneak," the tiefling says. "But Nylas tromps about here like an elephant."

"Otherwise he'd probably have killed you himself, right?"

The tiefling turns and glares at you with bright-red eyes. "So," she says. "What's it going to be?"

Get rid of her. Turn to page 38 . . .
Talk to her. Turn to page 75 . . .

This sounds like a bad idea all around.

"I really don't want to get involved in this kind of drama," you tell Nylas.

He nods in understanding. "I see."

You're not sure that he does, but you don't much care. You try to shut the door to the room to end the conversation, but he thrusts his booted foot in the way.

That's when you realize that you're in trouble.

Before you can breathe, Nylas waves in your direction, and something swooshes through the open bit of doorway and knocks you backward. Whatever it was, you didn't even see it coming, and—worse yet—you still can't see it now.

"You made a terrible mistake," Nylas says as he swings the door fully open. "My deadly and invisible friends will see that you pay for it."

"I just didn't want to get involved!" you say as excruciating pain strikes you again.

Nylas laughs. "No, your mistake was thinking that you weren't involved already. I can't have you blabbing about my plans. It's better, I think, that you're no longer here at all. . . ."

The pain strikes you again and again—until there's no more pain at all.

THE END

You know for a fact that you can't trust Nylas. If he's willing to betray his classmates to someone he's never met, he's sure to sell you out even faster. On top of that, if he's actually a Red Wizard and not just some pretender wearing their colors, they have an unmatched reputation for evil and cruelty.

You're pretty sure that if you agreed to help the man, he'd zap you dead the first chance he got—right after he got what he wanted from you. You suspect the same would be true if you turned him down flat. There's only one option left.

"Thank you," you say, putting on your most innocent face. "I can't tell you how much I appreciate you helping out a newcomer like myself. That's awfully kind of you."

"I'm just trying to help out the entire institution," the man says, visibly relieved that you've decided to see things his way. Or at least that he won't have to kill you on the spot before you can rat him out about his plotting. "Those two tieflings are a threat to everything Halaster has built here over so many years. With them out of the way, this'll be a better academy for us all."

"And the fact that it helps both of us out?"

He flashes a savage, toothy smile at you. "That's a happy coincidence, to be sure."

He turns and gestures toward the hallway beyond. "Shall we get to work?"

"Of course," you respond.

As he turns his back to you, you reach into the pocket

where you keep your cosh—a leather bag filled with heavy balls of lead. It served you well on the streets of Waterdeep whenever you needed to take someone out quickly and quietly, whether for a mugging or something more serious, and you hope it'll do the same for you here. The moment Nylas turns his back, you pull out the weapon and whack him on the head with it.

The man keels over without even a sound of protest, and you can't help but smile at how well that went. In your experience, it's always best to take out a wizard as fast as possible, before they can even mutter a single syllable of a spell. Otherwise, you're just asking for trouble—and such trouble rarely comes with a second chance.

You glance down the hallway and breathe a sigh of relief when you don't see any witnesses to your assault. As quickly as you can, you reach down and grab Nylas by the ankles and start hauling him into your room.

Turn to page 30…

L ook," you start to explain. "I'm really sorry, but I don't have much of a choice here. Your life is in danger, and I'm not talking about from me. Someone here wants you gone. It'd be easier if you were to leave peaceably."

The tiefling listens with her head to one side and a wry smile on her face.

"And if I don't?" she replies, her hand going to her wand.

You realize then that you don't have much choice. If she's given the opportunity to pull that wand on you, you won't stand a chance of escaping here alive, let alone retrieving the book. You snap your blade from its scabbard, striking faster than a snake. The tip of it catches the tiefling's neck, and she falls to the ground, reeling in shock at the speed of your attack. She drops her wand and clutches at her nicked throat.

"I don't want to kill you," you tell her. "But I'm not about to let you work your magic on me."

"You'll pay for that," she growls, her eyes flashing with hate. "You strike me down, and I promise I'll come back to haunt you for the rest of the few days you'll have left."

That's a hard promise for anyone to keep, but looking at the tiefling, you don't doubt she could pull it off. Despite that, you keep the point of your sword on her.

"What sort of choice are you leaving me?"

She snarls at you, dashing your hopes. "It doesn't matter. You're already dead no matter what you do. You just don't know it."

With that, she leaps up and starts to spit a spell at you. You don't recognize what she's saying, but you can already feel her magic starting to reach into your mind. If you let her finish, she'll kill you for sure.

You don't want to kill anyone, but you don't want to die yourself, so you run her through, and she dies at your feet, the last bit of her spell frozen on her lips. Shaking, you wipe your blade clean and sheathe it once more.

Was Nylas lying to you? Have you made a place for yourself in the school? Or have you just committed a crime for which you're doomed to die?

Now that the deed is done, are you supposed to head back to your room and wait for Halaster to find you so you can report what you've done? Or is that just the best way to ensure the wizard destroys you for harming one of his students?

You decide to hunt down Nylas, so you head back to the dormitory hallway, hoping to find him in his room. As you slip into the hallway, though, a wild woman leaps out of one of the other rooms, screaming at you at the top of her lungs.

Turn to page 44 . . .

C ephalossk creeps you out, and the thought of lining up the mind flayer's next couple of meals disturbs you. But at least the creature won't be feeding on you.

I sense your hesitation. It isn't unwarranted. But if it's the thought of killing that's causing you to pause, then be assured I'd be happy whatever way you manage to get them away from the school.

He pauses and watches you intently as you continue to consider his offer, all the more tempting now that you know you have options other than to murder the prospective student.

I sense your decision. It's good to be working with you. Let's get started right away.

The mind flayer opens the door to his room and ushers you into the hallway beyond.

"No time like the present," you say. You wipe your brow in relief. The room was somehow stifling and chilly at the same time, and you're glad to be free of it.

Cephalossk points to a door up the hallway. *That's Spite's room. You should start looking for him there.*

"And where are you going to be?"

I'll remain in my room and await the result of your attempt to eliminate him. If you succeed, I'll aid you in your quest to find Halaster's spell book.

"You could help me first instead."

You'd flee the first chance you had.

"Fine," you concede. "Go hide in your room until I'm done."

The mind flayer slips back into his room and silently

closes the door behind him. You take a deep breath and then saunter casually over to the door Cephalossk pointed at. It's closed, but you can hear two people inside, chatting.

You knock on the door, and a half-ogre, whose head scrapes against the top of the frame, opens it.

"Yes?" she says in a low voice.

"I'm applying to be a student here," you say. "I thought I should introduce myself to the others."

"Let them in!" a voice says from behind Dumara, who makes a fine door all by herself.

She moves aside grudgingly, and you squeeze past her into the room beyond.

It's the same size and shape as the room Halaster put you in. There's an additional oversize bed shoved into a corner, which makes things a bit tighter, and a rolltop desk stuffed between the beds.

A boy just on the edge of adolescence bounds over from where he's been sitting, surrounded by books.

"I'm Spite!" he says with wild cheer. "So glad to meet you! You're here to register as a student too?"

Dumara grunts at the boy for his unbridled enthusiasm. You just nod at the kid. "Maybe. I hear good things about the school."

"It's all right, but there are all sorts of other cool things here too. I can't wait to see them!" says Spite.

"Like what?"

"Halaster's spell book!" he says with unrestrained glee. "It's a real legend around these parts. I mean, all wizards

have spell books. I have one of my own, and I'm sure you do too. But just imagine how many spells such an ancient and powerful wizard must have stuffed away in his spell book. It'd be enough to fill an entire library!"

"I hadn't thought of it that way," you admit.

"Well, I want to get my hands on it, even if only to flip through its pages for a bit. Can you help me?" Spite looks up at you with hopeful eyes.

"And how would I do that?"

You can't believe your luck. If you can help Spite steal the spell book, then you can just turn around and swipe it from him.

"He keeps it in a secret room, very well guarded. To get to it, I need someone to distract Wormriddle—she's the night hag who helps run the school. If you can do that for me, I'll do whatever I can to help you get into the school. Then we'll be best friends too!"

Dumara looms over you while Spite awaits your reply.

Try to convince Spite to leave. Turn to page 25 . . .
Work with Spite. Turn to page 92 . . .

The screaming woman looks exactly like the woman you killed, right down to the color of her horns!

"Murderer!" she shouts at you. "I know what you did, and you're not going to get away with it."

She waves her hands, and a wall of flame erupts all around you. Your clothing catches fire instantly, and the blaze envelops you in horrifying pain.

You fall to the ground and try to beat out the fire, but no matter how hard you smack at the flames, the bits that are left burn hotter, faster, and hungrier. Soon, the fight goes out of you, and you find yourself a smoking mess of agony.

As you breathe your last, the woman looms over you, still seething with fury at you. Nylas joins her.

"I'm so sorry for your loss, my dear Turbulence," he says as he puts a hand on her shoulder. "But at least you avenged the death of your twin sister."

She smacks his hand away. "Don't you dare touch me. I know you had something to do with this. You're lucky I don't kill you too."

THE END

Thanks for your help," you say to Violence as you stuff the spell book into a large pocket inside your coat. "We'd better get going."

"What about my sister?" she asks. "We can't just walk out of here without her."

"Of course not. I'll go back to the entrance and make sure the way out is clear. I'll wait for you both there."

Violence considers this for a moment and decides to go along with your plan. She heads for a doorway to the south and disappears through it. You chase off down the hallway to the right, back toward the entrance.

When you reach it, you keep right on walking, heading into the rest of Undermountain. It's a long way back to the surface, and your client in Waterdeep. You want to get there as fast as you can manage.

Just as you think you've put Dweomercore behind you, though, you hear Violence shout, "Hold it right there!"

You try to run, but you realize that your feet are stuck to the ground. There's nothing sticky on them, but you can't seem to make them move.

You turn around and try to draw your blade, but Violence snaps at you. "Stop!"

Now you can't move at all.

"You really think you could get away with betraying me?" Violence says as she walks closer. "I'm a wizard too, you know." She stands behind you and whispers in your ear. "You're going to go back inside the academy and light a candle. Then you're going to walk through the place and set everything flammable that you can find on fire."

You find that you can't resist the compulsion to do exactly as she says.

"Please, no!" you beg her even as you begin walking back toward the school.

"I need a distraction to get my sister free," she says. "And if you're not going to help me honorably, you'll help me this way instead."

You scream in protest right up until Halaster finds you and lances you through with a lightning bolt. Before you can even try to explain, the shock fries you dead.

THE END

All right," you tell Violence as you stuff the spell book into a large pocket in your coat. "I need a spell or something to distract Halaster while you go and get your sister."

"Take this." She pushes a crystal into your hands.

Then she leans in and whispers a short incantation in your ear. You quickly commit it to memory.

"What'll it do?" you ask.

She simply smiles knowingly at you, then slips off down the hall. Realizing that there's little else for you to do at this point, you head toward the school's entrance, hoping that your presumed attempt at leaving will draw Halaster to you. Your instincts couldn't be more right.

"My apologies," he says as he rushes to meet you at the door. "I didn't realize you'd be so impatient."

"Not at all," you assure him. "I was just coming to find you. I wanted to show you what I can do."

"So eager," the Mad Mage responds with an amused smile. "Please, go ahead."

With that, you hold the crystal out in front of you and chant the magic words. The crystal starts to thrum in your hand and lets out a musical note you think sounds quite pretty. But as you finish, Halaster's face drops, and he moves to take the crystal from you. Too late. The quite beautiful musical note has turned to a piercing, high-pitched cacophony that makes you cover your ears. In doing so you drop the crystal, and the noise stops.

Turn to page 81 . . .

You pursue Medley into the smoke, following her by the sound of her cackles.

"Right this way!" she says.

When you emerge from the smoke, you find yourself in a laboratory of horrors. Four humanoid bodies lie under stained and dirty sheets, and a fifth sits off to the side in pieces, with only a single leg fully stitched together. Other bodies in various states of dismemberment hang from hooks along the far wall.

As you gag on the stench and gape at the horror of it all, Medley slams the door behind you and shouts, "Get him, my pretties!"

The creatures under the sheets rise and come at you—dead bodies torn apart and stitched back together into horrible mockeries of actual people. They have no weapons, but they look strong enough to not need to worry about such things.

You draw your blade and leap at the closest one, cutting, stabbing, and slashing as best you can.

While you might never have had a chance to prevail against so many creatures—much less Medley, whoever she really is—at least you go down fighting. As you breathe your last, you tell yourself that'll have to be enough.

THE END

While your client may have offered you a good deal of money to steal Halaster's spell book, no amount of money is worth risking your life among such a cutthroat bunch of students. If you stay here any longer, you might not survive to enjoy that reward.

You offer the man a regretful frown. "I'd love to join you here," you tell Halaster, "but I've taken a vow against violence. I only harmed this man in self-defense. If I have to manage that every day that I'm here . . ."

Halaster gives you an appraising look, unsure of what to make of you. He's clearly not used to having anyone turn down such an offer.

"You handle yourself pretty well for someone who's renounced violence."

"That's one of the things I hate most about myself," you lie.

"Fair enough," Halaster says as he gives Nylas's unconscious form a halfhearted kick. "Too bad we'll be stuck with him instead, though."

The Mad Mage ushers you out of the academy, leaving you to your long journey back to Waterdeep. You wonder how you're going to explain this to your client, but at least you'll have the chance.

THE END

After several weeks at the school, you make a series of unbelievable discoveries that cause you to change your plans entirely. At one point, you walk into the headmaster's office and discover him talking to himself.

In this case, it's not just Halaster muttering under his breath or speaking to a mirror. Instead, it's Halaster chatting with a whole other Halaster sitting across from him at the desk. You freeze and hope that you might be able to slink away without them noticing you, but the way they both turn and glare at you dashes that hope instantly.

"Come on in," the Halaster behind the desk says to you. "Convince us that we shouldn't kill you."

You do as ordered and stand before them, trying not to break down in fear. "Because I'm your best student. And you can't maintain this charade forever."

The Halaster sitting in front of the desk laughs at your bravado. "Go on."

You point at the man sitting behind the desk. "The real Halaster must be too busy to bother with drilling stubborn young wizards on how to cast his favorite cantrips." You point at the other man. "You, on the other hand, clearly aren't the real Halaster but someone who's posing as him to get wizards to study at this school."

"I told you he was smart," the imposter says to the other wizard. "Maybe too smart."

The real Halaster laughs out loud. "I'm not afraid of smart people. Isn't that why we started this school after all? To find the smartest upcoming wizards in the world and indoctrinate them onto our side?"

"That's kind of brilliant," you say with a nod. "The only people who have a real chance of taking you down and destroying everything you've built here are wizards, right? So keep them as close to you as you can." You gesture toward the imposter. "Without doing any of the work yourself."

The imposter drops his disguise, transforming into a humanoid creature who looks like a man-sized fox.

"It's a reasonable arrangement for a demon like me. I get to mold the minds of the next generation of wizards, and I can call on the greatest wizard of the age for help whenever I need it."

"And you never get tired of that?" you ask, sensing a potential opportunity. "How long have you been doing this?"

The imposter gives Halaster a sidelong glance. "It's not a burden."

"But maybe there are times when you'd like a break? A chance to wander the world and do something different."

The imposter squirms in his chair. "Most days here are pretty good."

Halaster narrows his eyes at you. "What are you suggesting?"

You give him a nonchalant shrug, as if the idea just occurred to you. "If you have one person impersonating you here, why can't you have two?"

Halaster and the imposter give each other meaningful looks, then the Mad Mage nods at you. "How can we trust you to keep our secret?"

"I assume you'll murder me and everyone I told."

"See?" Halaster says. "You are smart."

After that fateful meeting, you work even harder on your studies. Eventually, Halaster allows you to step in for the demonic imposter from time to time. One day, the demon doesn't bother to return.

Now that you're in the fold, you discover that Halaster has several spell books, and the one that he keeps at the academy is the least of them, a decoy left as a lure for thieves. You wonder if you should take revenge on the person who sent you here to steal it, risking your life for something worthless. Then you realize that they did you the greatest favor of your life. Without them, you might have died trying to explore Undermountain with a team of underpowered adventurers. Instead, you now run the best wizards' academy in the world.

Not bad for a thief from Waterdeep. Not bad at all.

THE END

W hat other choice do you have? After all, getting into the school—weird as it might be—is exactly why you came here, isn't it?

"I accept," you say, still unsure that you're doing the right thing.

Halaster gives you a smile you can only interpret as hungry. No matter how uncomfortable it makes you, though, you realize that you're committed to this course of action.

"Excellent. Welcome to my academy. I hope you'll be with us for a long time."

You glance down at Nylas, who's still unconscious on the floor.

Halaster chuckles. "Longer than him, at least."

You settle into the life of a student after that, constantly on the lookout for a way to find and steal Halaster's spell book. The entire time, Halaster, the rest of the academy's staff, and the other students all watch you like hawks, giving you zero chance to accomplish your mission. Rather than expose yourself as a fraud, you throw yourself into your studies, biding your time.

To your own disbelief, you discover you have some talent for magic. You think you might actually have a career ahead of you as a wizard.

Turn to page 51…

S top," the boy demands. Except, when you look around the oni at him, he's no longer a boy but a white-bearded man. "I think it's the truth."

"Do you think we've been found out?" Dumara asks him over her shoulder. "If so, we need to get out of here."

"Not yet. Not until we get what we came for," Spite replies. "But what to do with this one in the meantime?"

Dumara raises a clawed hand and cocks an eyebrow in question. Spite studies you further as you quiver against the door.

"If it's the spell book you're after, I could help you steal it," you offer, though you're unsure what you could bring to the party that neither of these can already offer. Or, for that matter, how you'd get the book off them later to deliver to your employer.

Spite considers your quivering form and sighs. "Just go," he says. "You should probably get out of here before you get yourself in more trouble than you can handle."

You don't need to be told twice. Twisting the handle, you pull the heavy door open and sprint from the room. Straight into the waiting tentacles of Cephalossk.

"Thought you could double-cross me, eh?" he says as he squeezes you, blocking off your air supply. "No worries; at least I can have a fresh dinner tonight."

THE END

I f Halaster's spell book is behind that door, then I don't need your help to find it," you tell Violence, who gawks at your bold betrayal.

Your conscience nags at you, but not badly enough to make you change your mind. You have a job to do, and helping a couple of young wizards to escape from someone only marginally more evil than them isn't part of it.

"Good luck to you and your sister, but you're on your own."

You push past the shocked tiefling, and she doesn't raise a finger to stop you. You glance around to make sure no one else is looking. Then you crack open the thick oaken door and slip through into the room beyond.

This puts you in an entryway that faces onto a round room with a high ceiling. A set of pneumatic tubes stands against the left wall, and a wide desk stretches across the far side of the room. A life-size statue of Halaster looms over a tall, ornately carved chair sitting behind the desk.

Before you even have a chance to start looking for the spell book, the door slams behind you, making a sound as loud as a crack of thunder. You spin around, realizing you've made a terrible mistake. There aren't any other exits from the room, and you just left an angry tiefling outside the only door.

"Mess with me, will you?" Violence shouts through the door. "You think you can get away without paying a price? How about you pay this price!"

"Wait!" you say, hoping you can talk her out of

whatever she has planned—which you're sure won't end well for you.

She ignores you and starts screaming at the top of her lungs. "Help! Help! There's an intruder here, and he's broken into the headmaster's office!"

You try the door, but she's jammed it from the other side. It doesn't budge.

There has to be another way out of the place. As you move into the round room, you see that the chair is covered with screaming faces, and they somehow launch into an unholy choir of agony that sounds even worse than Violence's incessant screeching.

You fall to your knees, trying to block out the noise, but it seems to go right through the hands covering your ears. There's no escaping it. Not until Halaster flings the door open and finds you in his office.

"I thought I told you to wait for your entrance exam," the Mad Mage says as he storms into the room. You realize that you can hear him, which means all the screaming has somehow stopped.

"That tiefling tricked me," you tell him, hoping you can lie your way out of this. "She shoved me in here and started screaming about me trying to rob you!"

Halaster arches a doubtful eyebrow at you. "A tiefling, you say? Do you know which one?"

"Violence. She said her name was Violence."

The man frowns as he escorts you out of his office and sits you down at the desk where Violence once sat. A

wizened old woman with dark-blue skin and sharp, vicious teeth dashes in, the mummified skull of a cat dangling from the end of her necklace. A night hag if ever you've seen one.

"I'm taking a head count," she says, throwing her hands into the air. "I'm missing two of our students."

"Turbulence and Violence?" Halaster asks in a disappointed tone.

"Just the ones! They've been eyeing the exits for weeks. I think they might have taken advantage of this"— she points at you, flustered —"distraction and fled!"

"So does that mean there's room for me here, then?" you ask, trying to put a brave spin on it.

The night hag rubs her hands together and bares her teeth at you. "Yes, but I'm afraid not as a student. You'll be a lot more useful in my laboratory. I always need another warm body."

"To help run your experiments?" you say with a nervous swallow.

"No." She shakes her head. "As one of my subjects. . . ."

THE END

You, Spite, and Dumara walk along the hallway and reach a room where there's a door marked "Headmaster's Office — Knock Please." You wonder if the spell book you're after might be in there, but Spite leads you straight past it.

The door to the room is ajar, and you pause just for a moment to peer through it. You see Halaster himself sitting at a large desk, scribbling something on a scroll with a long-feathered quill. He pauses in his work for a moment, and you hurry on before he looks up to see you.

"All right, here's the plan," Spite says as he leads you through a set of doors and then straight through a wall that gives way in front of you as if it's not even there. "I'm going to take you straight to Wormriddle's private chambers. All you have to do is go in there, find her, and keep her occupied for a bit."

"You don't think Halaster's going to stop you if you march into his office and try to take his book?"

Spite snorts. "He has a spell book in his office, but that's just a decoy. I'm after the real thing. He keeps that in a far more secret place."

You walk right through another wall and find yourself in a wide hall. At the end of it, you can see a ghostly figure that looks as if it's searching for something on the far wall.

"Ignore it," Spite says without breaking stride. "It's another illusion."

He leads you right up to the image, and the ghost doesn't seem to notice you at all. She just continues examining the wall.

Spite turns to the right and spreads his arms toward a set of doors. "This is Wormriddle's place. You keep her busy, and Dumara and I'll take care of the rest. Good luck!"

The boy and his half-ogre friend hustle back down the hallway and disappear into a passageway on the left.

Sneak after Spite. Turn to page 73 . . .
Enter Wormriddle's quarters. Turn to page 68 . . .

That's the most ridiculous deal I've ever been offered," you say with a sad shake of your head. "And I let someone hire me to come here and steal the Mad Mage's spell book."

Violence goggles at you. "You don't believe me?"

"Not any more than I believed Nylas when he told me I should kill you so I could have your spot in the school. You should be grateful I'm such a skeptic."

The tiefling crosses her arms over her chest and frowns. "The difference is that I'm not lying."

"So you say, but I haven't lived this long by trusting people who tell me I can trust them."

She glares at you. "And if I start screaming for help?"

"Now, why would you want to do that? Just let me be on my way. Maybe I'll get into enough trouble on my own to provide a distraction you and your sister can use to escape."

She gives you a dubious shrug but then steps aside. "Fine," she says. "I hope you get into a fatal amount of trouble."

"It's been a pleasure meeting you too."

You open the doors behind her and slip through them, leaving Violence to mutter angrily at your dismissal. Finally free from anyone watching over your shoulder, you set to finding Halaster's spell book as fast as you can. If anyone else spots you, you can just claim that you're lost — or so you hope.

The hallway beyond stretches into the darkness, its high ceiling held up by thick columns of carved stone. As you reach the doors at the end of the hall, you hear the sound of a fight on the other side. You crack the doors open, and beyond you see Violence fighting three other wizards, including Halaster himself!

You glance backward, wondering how she could have possibly gotten past you, much less how she could already be losing a spell battle like this. Then you notice that she's somehow switched her robes to an entirely different color.

This can't be Violence. It must be the twin sister she was taking about, Turbulence.

Turn to page 71...

All right," you tell Violence. "You have a deal. Help me get that spell book, and I'll help you and your sister get out of here, in whatever way I can."

"You're smarter than you look," the tiefling says with a smile.

Before you can figure out just how insulted you should be, she turns toward the door marked "Headmaster's Office — Knock Please." "Follow me," she says.

You don't want to start a fight with your new partner in crime, so you do as she orders. She steps up to the door while you check the corridor to make sure no one's watching. Apparently satisfied that the way is clear, she opens the door and pulls you inside after her.

You find yourself in a round room with a tall vaulted ceiling. A set of fifteen pneumatic tubes lines the left-hand wall. Across from you sits a wide desk with a tall chair behind it. A statue of Halaster looms behind that, looking down at you with a stern glare.

As you move into the room, you see that the chair is covered with carvings of mouths flung open and screaming. You start to hear them screeching in your ears, but Violence silences them with a sharp word and a flick of her wand.

"There," she says. "That'll keep that nasty thing quiet, but we'll have to move fast. My spell will only last for a minute."

"I've robbed a noble's villa in less time than that," you say as you start searching the room.

As is your way, you carefully rifle through the desk,

but there's nothing like a spell book there. However, the wall opposite the pneumatic tubes is suspiciously bare.

You move over to inspect it and find a hidden catch. As you pull on it, a section of the wall swivels away, revealing a smaller round room. Overstuffed bookshelves line its walls all the way to the ceiling.

Violence gasps in surprise and delight. When she tries to rush into the room, you block her way with your arm.

"We're in a hurry!" she says.

"We need to be careful," you point out. "You really think that chair out there is Halaster's only protection for something as valuable as his spell book?"

"Good point." Violence waves her wand, and the floor of the room in front of you—which is mostly covered with a rug—begins to glow.

"That looks bad," you say. "But we can work our way around it."

You reach out and grab the edge of a bookshelf. From there, you swing yourself into the room and place your feet on a lower shelf, keeping yourself off the floor as if it were made of lava.

"Oh!" Violence says. She waves her wand over the bookshelves, and one particular volume on the other side of the room begins to glow. "That must be it!"

With your goal in sight, you move faster, crawling across the bookshelves like a gigantic spider. When you reach the book, you snatch it up, then rush back toward the door. As you near it, you can hear the chair begin to screech again.

"Quickly!" Violence says as she ushers you toward the door.

You don't need her to rush you away. The screeching chair is doing a fine job of that.

Once you're outside, Violence slams the door behind the two of you, and the chair—having accomplished its mission—shuts up.

You lean against a wall so that you don't collapse in relief, then open the book to see what you found.

The pages are blank.

"Is this a trick?" you ask Violence, wondering if she's betrayed you.

"Yes," she says with a chuckle. "But it's one Halaster likes to play. He writes in invisible ink. Your client will have to reveal it with magic."

You shoot her a dubious look, still unsure if you can trust her. If you bring this book to your client and it's useless, you'll be lucky if you're only laughed out of Waterdeep.

Leave without helping Violence. Turn to page 45...
Live up to your end of the bargain. Turn to page 47...

As Spite scampers off, you decide to go along with his plan for now. Let him deal with the risks of robbing Halaster himself. You can always steal the spell book from the young wizard later.

As you throw open the doors to Wormriddle's chamber, you plan to announce yourself loudly so that she can't possibly ignore you. You expect to see someone's living quarters beyond, or perhaps an office crammed full of books and papers. Instead, all you see is a wall of smoke or mist so thick and cloying that you can't peer beyond the doorway. Oddly, none of the befouled air seems to curl beyond the threshold of the chambers to spill into the hallway where you stand.

"Hello?" you call tentatively.

You wait a moment for an answer, but it doesn't come. The smoke trapped inside the room seems harmless — or at least not toxic — so you plunge in.

Inside the swirling smoke, you can just see past the ends of your outstretched arms but no farther. You wander around, blindly reaching out with your fingers, hoping that this behavior keeps you from running into a trap or whatever kind of fire might be causing all the smoke. Fortunately, the smoke doesn't seem to make you cough, although your eyes water.

"Wormriddle?" you finally say. "I'm looking for someone named Wormriddle. Are you here?"

"Who's asking?" a voice calls through the smoke.

You're so excited to hear someone else's voice that you

nearly charge straight after the sound, but caution grabs you first and slows you down.

"I'm a new student here at the academy," you say. "Well, at least I hope to be. And I thought I should introduce myself to the people running the place."

You spy the bright silhouette of an open doorway in front of you, and you steer your way toward it.

"Come in! Come in!" the voice says, and you follow it through the doorway.

Amazingly, the smoke stops at the threshold of this door as well. As you enter, tiny bones crunch under your feet. They cover the floor of the wide room from one side to the other, and there's no way to avoid them.

A large four-poster bed sits to your right as you enter. Mummified cats line the edges of the canopy that hangs over the filthy, moldy pillows and blankets.

On the wall above the bed, a line of crudely made dolls sits on a shelf. One of them looks an awful lot like Spite.

There's a young halfling with curly black hair sweeping the room. She greets you with a wide and eager smile.

"Why, hello, new student!" she

says with a gentle curtsy. "My name's Medley. What can I do to you? For you!"

"I'm looking for someone named Wormriddle," you say as you peer around the oddly furnished room. "I've never met her before, but Spite Harrowdale suggested I introduce myself to her before I take my entrance exam for the school."

Medley raises her eyebrows in surprise. "He did, did he? That Spite is quite the tricky one, he is. I suppose I shouldn't be surprised about that. Not at all."

"Can you help me find her?" you ask, suddenly uneasy.

You're not sure if your unease is because of how oddly the halfling is looking at you or because you're afraid that if you don't find Wormriddle soon, the night hag will discover Spite's plot. If that happens, the whole plan is shot.

"Why, I'd be delighted!" Medley says as she leans her broom against a wall and dusts off her hands. "Just follow me."

She steps into the smoke-filled chamber again. You can't see her, but she's cackling loudly enough that you're sure you can find her by the unsettling sound.

Refuse Medley's offer. Turn to page 4 . . .
Follow Medley. Turn to page 49 . . .

I surrender!" Turbulence shouts, raising her hands above her head.

As soon as she does, Halaster and the other two wizards stop dead in their tracks. They each move into a separate alcove at the edge of the room and stand atop a short pedestal, where they turn into statues.

Smiling at your luck, you slip silently into the room. Hurt and panting as hard as she is, Turbulence doesn't hear you. You spot an open archway leading into a hall to your right and duck into it fast.

Stalking quietly through the hallways and rooms, you hunt for anything that might resemble a powerful wizard's spell book, but you come up empty. One wildly impossible room you pass through seems to be part of a noble's villa basking under the warm Waterdeep sun, but you know better than to be fooled by such illusions.

Eventually, you come to a room that's occupied by a creature you can't just sneak past. You recognize it as a nothic, a gray-skinned, long-armed, ridge-backed creature with a massive single eye in the center of its face. It's chained to the floor, and it's wearing a helmet studded with large blue and red crystals.

It looks up as you crack open the door and softly squeaks, "Help?"

Free the nothic. Turn to page 78...
Slip past the nothic. Turn to page 84...

Dealing with Wormriddle seems like a bad idea. If she were that easy to distract, Spite would have had Dumara handle the task instead. Besides, you're not here to get into the school. You want that spell book!

You pad down the hallway after Spite and Dumara, moving as silently as you can and taking care to remain out of their sight. You follow them through a series of classrooms and then a supply room guarded by a couple of spectators: large floating eyeballs with four prehensile stalks that end in smaller eyes. A sign on the shelves reads, "Don't remove supplies without Headmaster Blackcloak's written consent."

The spectators watch you closely but don't move against you as you leave. You find yourself in a long, bent hallway, and follow it to the right until you come to a door. Beyond that is a large room, in the center of which is a well that, as far as you can tell, leads down to the next level of Undermountain. On the other side there's another hallway, where you hear Spite's footsteps stop.

You peer around the corner and see both Spite and Dumara duck into an alcove toward the end of the hall. A moment later, Dumara emerges with Halaster right behind her. The two of them head for a door at the end of the hall and disappear through it.

Suspicious, you pad up to the door and listen at it for a moment. Clearly, that wasn't Halaster you saw. It had to be Spite in disguise. But why would he have to masquerade as the headmaster?

Is there something in the next room that would attack

anyone who wasn't there with Halaster? Should you disguise yourself as Halaster too? You don't have the magic for that, but you're pretty handy with more mundane means of masquerade.

But if you show up as Halaster and Spite shows up as Halaster, is that going to confuse things and cause problems instead? You're not sure what to do. You only know that Spite and Dumara are getting farther away by the second.

Disguise yourself as Halaster. Turn to page 82...
Don't bother with a disguise. Turn to page 86...

Your fellow student Nylas brought me here to kill you," you tell the tiefling. "He says it's the only way to open a space for me at this school. But I'm willing to entertain the idea that he might have been lying."

The tiefling spits on the ground in disgust. "And they say that *my* people are fiends. Nylas has done more harm to people here in the few weeks I've known him than my twin sister and I have done in our entire lives."

"Is what he said true?"

She glares at you. "And what if it is? Does that mean you're actually going to try to kill me now?"

"Would I really have a chance?"

"Let's not find out." She shakes her head at you. "Nylas isn't entirely wrong. He's pulled this stunt before, and it worked out just like he said. Halaster likes to pit the students against one another."

You glance around the room. "Why?"

"He says he does it to make us tougher. To transform us into the kinds of wizards who have a chance to survive out there in the real world."

"But you don't believe that." You can tell from her tone.

"I think Halaster set up this school as a kind of fly trap for wizards. He tells you that he's going to make you into one of the greatest wizards of all time, but instead he uses this place to distract us from real studies, the kinds of things that might make us a challenge to him."

"You think this whole place is just a scam?" A part

of you is impressed that someone as powerful as the Mad Mage would go to such elaborate lengths to sucker people into studying with him.

But doesn't that make more sense than the idea that an all-powerful wizard who controls Undermountain would take the time to set up a school of wizardry? Out of the goodness of his heart?

"I just want to leave and bring my sister with me." She lets loose a sigh so deep, her shoulders slouch from the effort. "But Halaster isn't about to let that happen. Not without a fight — and that's a fight we can't win."

"I don't want to be a student here either," you tell her. "Maybe we can help each other out."

"How do you mean?" she asks, both suspicious and hopeful at the same time.

You hesitate, weighing what it would mean to bring someone in on the real purpose of your presence here. Maybe she could help, but maybe she'd just stab you in the back and take the book for herself. You decide to risk it.

"I'm here to steal Halaster's spell book."

"You're not a wizard?" she asks, surprised.

You shake your head. "I'm a thief. Someone hired me to steal the book. I just need to find it and get out of here."

"Would you be willing to take my sister Turbulence and me with you?"

"Your sister's name is Turbulence?" you ask. "What is yours?"

"Violence," she answers. You're not sure what to make

of that. They sound dangerous, but what else can you do?

"If you can help me, then I don't see why not. Though I'm not sure what I can offer that the two of you couldn't do for yourselves."

She considers this for a moment before giving you a serious nod. "All right," she says. "Let's do it. We can worry about the logistics of getting out of here later."

"Okay," you concede. "Where to?"

Violence points at the door in a corner of the room. "That's Halaster's quarters. His spell book has to be hidden in there."

"If you say so." This seems a little too easy to you.

Violence senses your hesitation and frowns at you. "You swear to me that you'll help us get out of here? You have to give me your word."

"You'd take the word of a thief you just met?"

"At this point, I don't see how we have much choice."

If the spell book's right here, you're not sure you need Violence's help. On top of that, there's always the chance she might be lying to you. Maybe the spell book's not there at all. Or maybe she'll try to take it for herself.

Push past Violence into Halaster's quarters. Turn to page 56 . . .
Ignore Violence and move on. Turn to page 62 . . .
Accept Violence's deal. Turn to page 65 . . .

You can't stand to see anything enslaved, even something as disturbing as a nothic. Legend has it that nothics come into being when wizards delve too deep into arcane studies and become irrevocably twisted by their own ambitions. You wonder if that's how this particular creature came to its fate. Was it one of Halaster's own students?

You put up your hands to show that you wish the creature no ill as you step into the room. It allows you to approach, and you see that the chain is attached to a collar around its neck. You pull out your thieves' tools and have the lock picked open in no time.

The nothic pulls off its helmet and smiles up at you with its long, sharp rows of teeth.

"Thank you," the creature says as it rubs the long-chafed skin on its neck. "I'm Halaster's secretary. He keeps me trapped here to handle the messages other wizards send him telepathically."

"That sounds horrible."

The nothic nods at you. "I read your mind, by the way. I know why you're here."

You brace yourself for the creature to attack you or start screaming for help. Instead, it frowns at you.

"Unfortunately, the Halaster who runs this school is an imposter. The real Halaster doesn't keep his best spell book anywhere near here."

You gape at the nothic. "You have to be kidding!"

"Many people have tried to steal Halaster's spell books over the years. They all failed, but they keep trying. You were probably sent here as a ploy."

"How do you mean?" you ask, confused.

"I imagine your attempt is supposed to draw the real Halaster to the academy so that someone else can try to steal his real spell book while he's not in his real home."

You clench your fists in fury. All the effort you went through to get here, all the dangers you faced—was that just so your client could sacrifice you like a pawn?

"We should leave now," the nothic says. "Halaster'll come to check on me soon."

"I'm going back to Waterdeep," you tell the creature. "As dangerous as that might be."

"Then why are you going back?" it asks.

You flash a dangerous smile. "Revenge."

THE END

Y ou look up sheepishly at Halaster.

"For you to fumble on such a simple spell, I think it's quite clear that there's no place for you here." He scowls. "My academy is for the best of the best, and this only goes to show that you don't fit that caliber."

You never wanted to join the school, and yet his scolding strangely hurts you. Slumping your shoulders, you leave without a word, bolstered only by the fact that you do so with the book in your pocket.

You're already halfway back to Waterdeep when Violence and her sister Turbulence catch up to you.

"You got away that easily?" you ask.

Violence nods. "That spell broke every piece of glass in the entire academy. It's a lot easier to slip out when everyone is busy worrying about what might explode next."

Turbulence smiles. "Perhaps we'll see you around."

"Perhaps."

You manage to get back to the surface and head to the Yawning Portal. Your client arrives soon after, finding you already finishing up the best meal you've had in weeks. She inspects the book carefully.

After a nervous moment, she nods. "I'd be surprised if this was Halaster's primary spell book, but it's certainly one of his." She throws a large purse full of coins on the table.

"All right," you say to the rest of the adventurers in the Yawning Portal. "The fun tonight is on me!"

THE END

If Spite went to the trouble to look like Halaster, then perhaps you should do the same. Fortunately, in the course of your career, you've become a decent disguise artist in your own right. It's a lot easier to walk into a place in a mask than it is to climb in through a window, after all.

You dig through your pack and find a white wig and a beard and slip them on. It's a good thing so many male wizards stick with that kind of look as they get older.

The hair alone won't be enough to fool anyone, though, so you also don a mask to cover your skin to make you look more like Halaster: old and wizened by years. It takes longer than you'd like, but eventually you feel you've done the best you can.

In an effort to catch up with Spite and Dumara, you bolt through the doors at the end of the hall and discover another hall that turns to the right. You follow it into a large square room with a statue of Halaster standing in each corner. If the statues bear a passable resemblance to Halaster, then it seems your own efforts are at least not likely to embarrass you. Even if Halaster's best friend were to discover you looking like this, you feel you might be able to fool him — at least on a dark, moonless night.

You glance around but don't see Spite or Dumara anywhere. There's only one other way out of the room, through a passage just to the right of the one by which you entered. Unless there's a secret exit elsewhere, that must be how they left.

Worried that you might have already lost the pair of

them for good, you decide to chance the passageway, and you slink up it quietly as it winds off to the right. Moving faster, you turn a corner just in time to see Halaster—Spite in disguise, for sure—follow Dumara through a door into a well-lit room. The door closes behind them, and you sidle up to it and wait.

At least they haven't gotten entirely away from you, but chasing them straight into the room would only ensure that they catch you following them. Forcing yourself to be patient, you start counting to one hundred to give them a moment to move on or—if they're stopping there—to become engrossed in whatever it is they've found. Then you plan to peek through the door and see what's happening, hopefully without giving them a chance to spot you in the act.

That's when you hear someone inside the room start to scream, and all your plans get tossed away.

You consider waiting until the screaming stops, at which point you could enter the room and maybe just pick through the mess and move on. But your curiosity gets the better of you.

Turn to page 89...

It's awful to see anything enslaved like this nothic, but you don't have time to lend it a hand right now. You need to press on.

With a cautious narrowing of your eyes, you give the chain holding the creature's collar a good, hard look. You might be able to squeeze past the nothic if you press your back flat against the wall. As you make your way toward the door on the opposite end of the room, though, you discover that you forgot to consider the reach of the nothic's abnormally long arms!

It grabs you in a steely grip and pulls you close to its wide-open jaws. Before it can clamp its pointy teeth into your flesh, though, you manage to draw your blade and run the creature straight through.

The nothic screeches in agony, then slumps over as you withdraw your sword.

"I'm sorry," you say as it crumples to the ground in front of you. "You didn't give me any choice."

The creature rolls over onto its back and stares up at you with its one huge eye. It begins to shudder softly, and you almost start to feel bad for it, when you realize that it's laughing.

"What's so funny?" you ask as a shiver lances straight down your spine like cold silver.

"You think you didn't help me, but you did," it says. "I wanted to be free of this place, and now I finally am. Free in death! But soon, soon you'll join me there."

The creature points to its ridiculous helmet. "I'm in

constant telepathic contact with Halaster. And I just let him know you killed his favorite servant."

Dismayed, you gape down at the creature as it draws its last cursed breath. You need to get out of here. Now!

Desperate, you push your way out of the room, going back the way you came. While you were wandering around, you thought you saw a garbage chute down to the next level. As you sprint toward it, though, there's a blinding flash of light, and then someone bellows at you in cold fury.

"How dare you!"

Turn to page 93 . . .

There's not enough time to throw on a proper disguise, or at least that's what you tell yourself. You open the door and move down a hallway that leads to the right. At the end of it, you find a large square room with a statue of Halaster standing in each corner. A single other passageway leads out of the room, through the same wall by which you entered.

You don't see a disguised Spite or Dumara anywhere, but you think you hear their footsteps up that other passageway. You're about to follow them at a safe distance when you're attacked.

Two human-sized creatures leap through the wall to your right as if it weren't even there. Another leaps through the wall to your left.

The ones on your right have thick gray carapaces, covered with ridges of spikes. They have large insect-like eyes, and their pincers snap and clack together over their hungry mouths. Each of the monsters carries a trident in the lower set of its four arms.

The creature on the left has green skin, long horns sprouting from its forehead, and a pair of leathery wings spreading from its back. It hoists a notched battle-ax as it approaches you. None of the creatures seems interested in conversation.

You turn to flee, but suddenly all the lights in the room go out. This has to be the effect of some sort of magical darkness, which means even if you could light a torch, it wouldn't do you any good.

Instead, you duck and dodge and try to sneak your way out of the room, but when one of the tridents stabs you in the side, you realize that the creatures attacking you can see in the dark just fine — even magical darkness.

If that's true, you're doomed. Despite that, you draw your blade and try to put up a fight, slashing out at unseen horrors in the darkness. When you strike something fleshy and elicit a bellow of pain, you smile, but your pleasure is short-lived.

The creatures soon knock you flat. As you lie dying, you realize that Spite got past them because he looked like Halaster, and you wonder if that would have saved you too.

THE END

You throw open the door and see that the screams are coming from Spite, who's being pulled up into the air and then slammed down onto the hard stone floor by an invisible force. It seems to be directed by a giant skull with blazing eyes set into a door on the far side of the room. Your first instinct is to charge in and attack the skull while it's busy with Spite.

Before you can manage that, though, a rough-hewn statue of iron steps in front of the door and reaches out to slam it shut in your face. A large blue-skinned creature—who oddly shouts in Dumara's voice—smashes into the moving statue, clawing at the metal thing with long and vicious black talons.

"Help us!" Spite shouts as he sees you.

You wonder for an instant if he thinks you're the school's headmaster, but he shatters that by telling you, "That's the worst disguise I've ever seen! How did you get past the yugoloths?"

You have no idea what yugoloths are, but perhaps it's better that way. Right now you have a decision to make. If you call for help, the whole caper is blown; if you don't, Spite might die. But maybe that's okay. . . .

Call for help! Turn to page 95 . . .
Wait to see what happens. Turn to page 108 . . .
Save Spite! Turn to page 98 . . .

"You look like someone who hates it here, right?" you say to the tiefling with the most charming smile you can muster. "I'm here to rob Halaster. Lend me a hand?"

She glances over your shoulder, and you look back in that direction as well. If Halaster's chasing you, he's taking his time.

"This way," she says furtively as she moves toward the door to the headmaster's office and cracks it open. "Quickly! And be careful in there!"

Without hesitation, you obey and slip past her into the room beyond. There's a short entryway, and beyond that it's round, with a domed ceiling high above. The left wall is lined with a strange set of tubes that lead into the ceiling and floor, and there's a desk on the far side of the room. A life-size statue of Halaster stands behind it, dressed in a long robe covered with dozens of eyes. It holds a staff atop which a heatless flame burns like a magical torch.

As you slink into the room to search for Halaster's spell book, the chair behind the desk begins to scream. It's impossible to tell exactly where the sound is coming from—the chair doesn't have a mouth anywhere on it—but the noise is enough to make you cover your ears and wince in pain. You cast about for the book for a moment, but you don't see it anywhere.

The chair must be some kind of magical alarm. You need to get out, fast!

When you emerge from the room, the tiefling tackles you to the ground.

"I've got the thief!" she shouts. "Help!"

You try to squirm away, but when you see Halaster storming down the hallway, you begin to panic.

"I tried to help you," the tiefling whispers, "but I'm not going to take the blame for you being a lousy thief!"

You squirm out of her grasp and stand up. As you do, you realize you've made another mistake. Now the wizard coming your way has a clear shot at you.

"Get away from my student!" Halaster says as he flicks his wand at you.

A bolt of lightning shoots right through you, frying you dead.

THE END

I'd be happy to help you out," you tell Spite. "Going on a spell book hunt sounds like a lot of fun."

"Oh, it'll be more than that," Spite says. "Just think of the things we'll learn!"

"But I'm not sure I have the time for it right now." You give Spite a reluctant shrug. "I mean, I'm supposed to be waiting to take the school's entrance exam."

Spite and Dumara look at each other and then break out laughing.

"Don't worry," Dumara says in a booming voice.

"There *is* no entrance exam," Spite says with a grin. "Halaster just waits for you to sneak out of your room and interact with the other students—which can be fatal. If you survive, you're in!"

That may be the craziest thing you've ever heard about any kind of school, but somehow you're not all that surprised. "All right, then," you say to Spite. "I'm in!"

"Excellent!" Spite trundles out the door with Dumara in his wake.

"Off we go on a grand adventure!" Spite says.

"Grand adventure!" echoes Dumara.

Turn to page 60...

You charge along at top speed, determined to outrun and outlast the master wizard. When you reach the entrance to the school, though, Halaster is there waiting for you.

"You can't outrun magic!" the man snarls.

"I didn't mean to hurt anyone!" you say.

"Oh, don't worry. I'm not going to hurt you." Halaster gestures at you with his wand. "I'll leave that to every other creature you have the misfortune of coming across, of which I suspect there will be many!"

A bolt flashes from the tip of the wand, and suddenly everything around you is much larger. It takes you a moment to realize that you've been shrunk to the size of a rat.

Halaster throws back his head to start laughing, and you use that instant to make your break.

As you race past the wizard and into the darkness, he calls after you. "Run, for all the good it'll do you! You won't get far."

You do your best to prove him wrong. It's a long trip back to Waterdeep, but most of the monsters don't even notice you sneaking past them. When you finally reach the city, though, it's the rats that finally spot you and put an end to you. There are just too many of them, after all.

THE END

H elp!" You turn and shout. "Help!"

"No, wait!" Spite calls through the still-open door as you race back down the hallway. "Don't leave us here."

The metal creature slams the door shut behind you, cutting off Spite's screams and Dumara's ferocious roars.

"Help!" You scream so loud you feel like you're shredding your throat raw.

When you reach the room with the statues of Halaster, you realize that no matter who you alert, it's probably going to be too late to help Spite and Dumara. Despite that, you keep running and shouting, trying to retrace your steps without getting lost.

At least you have the presence of mind to remove your disguise and stuff it back into your jacket. You hate to think how Halaster might react seeing you in it.

When it dawns on you that you've made a wrong turn in your panic, you double back to where you were before. At that point, you run—almost literally—into Halaster.

"My good fellow," he says, concern wrinkling his aged brow. "Whatever is the matter?"

"Spite! And Dumara! They're being killed!"

"By whom?"

You hesitate for an instant, knowing you might get in trouble for following Spite to the room where he was attacked. There's no way to change that now, though, and Halaster's bound to find out sooner or later anyhow.

"He was acting suspicious, and I followed him to a room where there was a giant metal creature and a skull on a door that seemed to be slamming him around."

Halaster grimaces as he nods. "The sanctuary. They'll be dead already."

"We have to do something!" You grab Halaster by the arm and pull him back toward the room. "Maybe there's still a chance."

Halaster lets you lead him along. When you reach the room with the statues of him in it, he frowns. "You got this far before? And you didn't see any yugoloths?"

Still unclear about what a yugoloth might be, you shrug helplessly. Halaster continues without pursuing the question further.

When you reach the door the metal creature slammed shut, Halaster opens it carefully. Cautiously, you peer over his shoulder to gaze into the room.

Everything seems perfectly calm. Both Spite and Dumara lie on the floor, dead. The skull on the door across the way seems perfectly normal—for a skull hanging on a door. Just a decoration. You crane your neck and spot the metal creature standing next to you, now still as a statue. It doesn't even move enough to look your way.

Halaster sighs and shuts the door. "We'll get that cleaned up later. I warn people time and again about entering private rooms like that, but every so often we run into someone who just can't be bothered to listen. And for that they pay the ultimate price."

He gives you a kindly look. "You're probably

wondering just how this tragedy affects you and your application to study at the academy."

"Honestly, it was the furthest thing from my mind," you respond.

Halaster begins to lead you back toward the main part of the school. "Well, in this case, Spite's horrible loss is your gain. His removal from our roster means that there's a brand-new opening for a promising student, and it seems clear by your actions that you'd be an excellent candidate."

You wince at this. While you certainly wanted to weasel your way into the school, it turns your stomach to think that someone had to die to make it happen.

Halaster senses your hesitation. "If you don't take the spot, it's not like we're going to hold it open in honor of Spite. It's just going to go to someone else eventually. What do you say?"

Take it. Turn to page 100 . . .
Politely decline. Turn to page 105 . . .

As foolish as it might be to stay, you can't just abandon Spite and Dumara to die. If you run for help, there's no way to get back to them in time either. There has to be something you can do to save them, here and now.

On an impulse you hope to live to regret, you slip into the room — just before the metal monster slams the door shut behind you. Now you're trapped in there with the others whether you like it or not.

The monster comes straight for you and swings a fist the size of a war hammer at your head. You dodge beneath it and scramble out of the way as fast as you can.

Dumara takes advantage of the monster's distraction and leaps onto its back, attempting to dismantle it. She tears at its shoulders, peeling plates off it with her bared claws. She even manages to rip off an arm and tosses it aside to clatter across the dungeon's stone floor.

The metal monster reaches back and grabs Dumara with its remaining arm, pulling her over its shoulder. It smashes her to the ground and begins to pound her.

Spurred into action, you leap at the monster from behind and shove your blade between two of the metal plates that cover its back. Rather than trying to stab it over and over again—which would seem like a useless way to attack a beast with no flesh—you use the blade as a lever and start trying to pry pieces of the creature away from its body. You wrestle off part of its side and then finally manage to wrench away its head, which bounces away from you with a series of hollow clangs.

This finally causes the creature to collapse into a pile of wreckage. Unfortunately, it crumbles to pieces right on top of Dumara, who wasn't doing all that well to begin with.

"Save Spite," Dumara says to you with her final breath.

You spin about and dive toward the boy just as he's about to crash into the floor again. On your knees, you catch him in your arms and cradle him there, giving him a chance to catch his breath.

Rather than take the time to thank you, Spite scrambles out of your arms and casts a spell on the skull, one that he's been trying to complete the entire time the thing has been battering him about. The skull goes dark and slack, and Spite nearly falls over in relief.

Turn to page 102 . . .

S tuck for a better solution than just walking away from the academy, you stick out your hand and tell Halaster, "I'd be honored to accept a position as a student here at your academy, and I look forward to studying the arcane arts under your guidance."

This is the furthest thing from the truth, of course, but in your mind it increases the chances of you walking out of the academy alive. After witnessing what happened to Spite and Dumara, that's the only thing you care about at the moment. Escaping with Halaster's spell book has fallen far down your list.

Halaster shakes your hand with a gentle smile. "Then some good has come out of this horror after all. I'll speak with Wormriddle and have you registered immediately. In the meantime, you can consider the dormitory room I showed you earlier your permanent quarters. Welcome to Dweomercore!"

The wizard doesn't seem all that dismayed by the fact that a boy has just been killed by a security system he supposedly set up himself. This alone you find rather disturbing. Add the fact that you could expect similar care about your own fate as one of his students, and it's downright terrifying.

Halaster guides you back to your room, calm as can be. "Just to make sure you don't somehow get lost again."

Given the circumstances, you interpret that as "to make sure you don't rob the school on your way out."

He leaves you at the door and tells you to get settled in

the room, which is now officially your new home.

"Get some rest," Halaster says. "We'll have a little ceremony at dinner tonight to welcome you to the academy and introduce you to your fellow students."

You thank him for his kindness and hospitality with as much gratitude as you can muster. Once he's gone, you shut the door behind him, then sit on the bed with your head in your hands as you contemplate your fate.

You're not sure exactly how you could have made a bigger mess of this. If Halaster thinks about it much longer, he's going to wonder how you could have made it through that room with the yugoloths—or whatever they were—without a disguise. And he might even come to believe that you set up Spite and Dumara to be killed.

Maybe that's not the kind of thing that Halaster discourages in this awful school of his, but either way, this is not the sort of place where you want to spend all that much time. You need to get out of here as fast as you can.

You wonder if you could somehow manage to get past the crazy skull and the metal monster that killed Spite and Dumara. If those two couldn't handle them, though, there's little chance you could deal with such creatures on your own. And even then, you're still not sure exactly where Halaster's legendary spell book might be. It's probably beyond that door in the room, but just getting through the door doesn't mean you could survive whatever else might be inside.

Turn to page 113 . . .

N o time to chat," Spite says. "We need to get that door open before the skull powers up again."

"I'm on it," you say.

You reach the door and see that it has nine separate locks. You examine them, hoping to pick the locks, but none of them feature a keyhole.

"They're magically locked," you say. "Each one of them requires a spell to open it."

"Step back!" Spite says as he points his wand at the door. He then rattles off a series of spells, each of which produces a knocking sound so loud you wonder if Halaster might be able to hear it in his quarters.

As the ninth spell sounds, you grab the door and haul it open. There's only a single desk and chair in the room beyond, both bare.

Spite pushes past you and rips open the desk's single drawer. "Found it!" he crows with glee.

As crazy as it might sound, this all seems too easy to you. Halaster wouldn't let just anyone pick up his spell book, right? But if you let Spite have it now, you might never be able to take it for yourself.

Let Spite have the spell book ... for now. Turn to page 118 ...
Grab the spell book. Turn to page 121 ...

The horror of the scene overwhelms you for a moment, and you become paralyzed with indecision about what to do. If you call for help now, you might be in serious trouble for allowing Spite and Dumara to die—no matter how sure you are that you couldn't have done anything to prevent it.

After pondering the situation for a bit, you realize that you really have only two choices. You can enter the room and try to steal the spell book, or you can leave Dweomercore immediately and return to Waterdeep empty-handed.

You don't like the idea of failing at your mission, but on the other hand, you absolutely hate the idea of being killed. If the things in that room could handle both Spite and Dumara, what chance do you realistically have against them alone?

Still, heading back to Waterdeep without anything to show for it? You've never suffered such a resounding defeat in your entire life. You're not sure you could bear it.

It's then that a third option dawns on you. You're in a magic school, surrounded by magical items and magical people. Surely there must be something or someone here that could help you find out what's behind that door. But then you might have to fight to keep possession of the book. Or worse, share your payment.

Look for something or someone to help. Turn to page 116...
Enter the room. Turn to page 110...

Declining Halaster's offer seems like the wise thing to do, but you hesitate, unsure how the mighty wizard will take to you turning him down. You're sure there are other wizards out there who'd literally kill to be his student.

"I'm sorry," you say, cringing as you speak. "But I can't. I'm sure you have lots of wonderful teachers and students here, and under other circumstances I'd be happy to join you. Accepting a position here because of the death of someone else, though, seems like a bad omen at the very least."

Halaster stares at you for a long moment, and you wonder if he's about to berate you for being an incredible idiot who's willing to insult one of the most powerful mages of the age. Then he breaks into a wide smile.

"You're a wise person," he says as he claps you on the shoulder. "I can't tell you how many others have accepted a position at this school and come to regret it in the worst possible ways."

You goggle at that. "Is it really that terrible here?"

Halaster shrugs, then motions for you to follow him back toward the school's entrance.

"The staff and I do our best to teach the students here what they need to know to survive in the outside world, but we don't do anything to protect them from one another."

"That seems . . . cruel." You can't find a better word for it.

"Perhaps it is," Halaster says with a chuckle. "But it's part of how we prepare them for the outside world. If they can't survive their rivalries within the school, there's a very good chance they'd fail just as miserably in the wider world."

You shake your head. You can't agree with such a philosophy, but it makes your decision to leave a lot clearer.

You walk in silence for a while. As you near the entrance, Halaster looks at you.

"Do you know what Spite was doing in that room?"

You were afraid the Mad Mage might ask you that question. Worried that he might see through an outright lie, you offer up a half-truth.

"He mentioned something about an all-powerful spell book. . . ."

Halaster snickers at that. "The little fool. To think he lost his life over something like that. And the life of his friend as well."

"You mean there's no such spell book here? With a wizard as powerful as you on the premises?"

Halaster grunts. "I'm an old man. Older than you could possibly grasp. I have spell books scattered all over the place, most of them locked up in safe places, deep in the heart of Undermountain. Well, not so safe for anyone who doesn't happen to be Halaster."

"And the ones you have here?"

Halaster favors you with a wan smile. "Not the best of the bunch by a long, long way. Between you, me, and the perpetual torches, they're not worth dying over."

When you reach the entrance to the school, Halaster bids you farewell and wishes you a safe journey back to the surface.

"I'd offer you an escort back, but that seems like it would be a waste of time for whoever I sent with you. If you made it this far down into Undermountain on your own, I'm sure you can survive the journey back."

As you depart Dweomercore and head for Waterdeep once more, you reflect upon this. Your client appears to have sent you on a dangerous quest for little in the way of reward. Were they expecting you to be killed in the process? If so, you might want to start plotting your revenge.

THE END

Much as you hate yourself for it, you don't think you can do much to save Spite and Dumara at this point. You hesitate just long enough for the metal creature to slam the door right in your face.

Maybe you could find someone to help, but you're pretty sure that Spite and Dumara would be long dead by the time you managed to locate anyone, much less bring them back here to do something about it. It's possible that when Spite entered the room he triggered some kind of alarm, in which case someone should be along shortly to stop the violence.

That doesn't happen. Instead, Spite keeps screaming until he falls utterly, horribly silent. Dumara roars in protest, but eventually that stops too.

Still no one has come. You cock your head and listen carefully. Not able to hear much, you step forward and press your ear to the door.

Somewhere in the room, you hear the sound of metal squeaking and scraping against metal as the creature moves across the floor to your left. There, it seems to hesitate for a moment as it settles into place. Then that sound stops too.

To be cautious, you wait a few minutes longer, just to make sure. Nothing happens. No one moves. No one besides you even breathes.

You try the latch. It moves easily, and you give the door a gentle push on its well-oiled hinges. It swings into the room.

Spite and Dumara lie spread out on the floor, beaten and mangled. They don't move a muscle.

The giant skull attached to the door on the opposite side of the room seems lifeless once more. Its jaw remains still, and there's no glow to its eyes.

Watching it carefully, you edge up to the doorway, making sure not to cross the threshold. Leaning into the room, you crane your neck to spy the metal creature standing there like a statue, guarding the door.

Turn to page 103 . . .

Maybe you were mistaken about the skull and what it was doing to Spite. If you move fast, you think you might be able to handle the metal creature. All you have to do is stay out of its reach, and you've proven pretty good at doing that with other foes over the years.

Steeling yourself, you draw your sword and flex your fingers around its hilt for a moment. Then you take a deep breath and charge into the room, heading straight for the door across the way.

As you pass the metal creature, it creaks to life. Rather than chasing after you, though, it moves toward the door you came through.

You get about halfway across the room when something in the skull on the door blazes, and you find yourself hoisted off your feet by an invisible force.

Unable to progress, you scream in terror and slash about in the air with your blade, but there's nothing close enough for you to hit. You consider throwing your sword at the skull, but you hear the metal creature lumbering up behind you.

Flailing about, you try to turn to face the oncoming monster, but that's when the invisible force throws you to the ground. It slams you into the stone floor hard enough to knock the breath from your lungs. You're still gasping for air when the metal monster kicks you in the ribs.

Before you can recover, the invisible force hauls you high up into the air again, too high for the metal creature to grab you. That doesn't save you, though, since the force slams you down again a few seconds later. The monster gives you another kick, starting the torturous cycle all over again.

Someone begins laughing from the doorway, and you manage to wriggle around enough to spot Halaster standing there, watching the monster and skull beat you to death.

"Help!" you scream.

"Sorry," Halaster says. "I can't."

Turn to page 119 . . .

If you're being honest with yourself, it looks like this entire mission is a bust. Unless you dedicate yourself to the study of magic long enough to figure out how to get past the defenses Halaster's set up around his spell book, it would be certain death to try to steal the thing. And is the payoff really worth so many weeks of your life?

You don't bother unpacking your gear. Instead, you head straight for the entrance to Dweomercore.

This whole trip doesn't have to be a complete loss, though, right? After all, you have to make your way back through eight levels of Undermountain before you reach Waterdeep, and you bypassed all sorts of interesting things on your path here. There has to be something worth stealing along the way. There might even be an adventuring party down here that needs the services of a skilled thief. . . .

THE END

You kneel next to Spite and gingerly take the spell book from his grasp. As you stuff it into a large pocket on the inside of your jacket for safekeeping, Spite's eyes fly open, and he reaches out to grab you by the wrist.

He tries to say something but just coughs instead.

"I'm sure someone will be here to help you soon," you tell him. "We made a lot of noise."

"Get out of here before the skull comes back to life, you idiot," Spite wheezes.

You leap to your feet. "Good luck," you say to him.

"I'm done for either way," he says. "I'd ask you to kill me on your way out if it wouldn't take too long."

He has a point, and you don't have any desire to hurt him. He's done enough of that to himself. You head for the door, racing past both Dumara and the broken remains of the metal monster scattered all over her.

"It's not fair," Spite calls as you leave him and the room behind.

You can't help but agree with him about that, but you've had plenty of bad luck in your life too. You're not about to argue when some good luck comes your way instead.

Quick as you can, you creep back to the hallway. Footsteps thunder toward you, so you duck into one of the niches there and hunker down in the shadows.

"This way," Halaster shouts after he passes you. "The master's going to be furious!"

You don't know what he means by that, but you're not

going to stop him to ask. Once he and the others have gone, you head for the entrance to the academy. You make it there without incident and bid Dweomercore goodbye.

Now you just need to get back to Waterdeep and collect your fee. When word of this gets out, your legend will surely grow!

THE END

There's no way you could face the threats in that room on your own. The metal monster would be enough to destroy you, even if it didn't have that crazy telekinetic skull on its side. The only thing to do is find something or someone to help. Turning your back on the room, you go in search of an ally.

When you emerge from the hallway into the room with the four statues of Halaster in the corners, though, you find the real Mad Mage standing there waiting for you.

"Where do you think you're going?" he says, peering at you with steely eyes. "And just who do you think you are, thief?"

You put your hand to your mouth to gasp in horror, and you feel an unfamiliar beard there. You realize that you forgot to remove your Halaster disguise before you got moving.

"I know this looks bad," you start.

"It looks like you were trying to break into the sanctuary to steal the spell book of Halaster Blackcloak. That's not just bad. It's outright stupid."

"I was just following Spite and Dumara here," you protest. "I didn't know what they were up to."

Halaster sneers at you. "That doesn't explain your ridiculous look. Are you supposed to be me? Did something that pathetic really fool my guards?"

You pull the mask and beard off and goggle at the wizard. "I saw Spite disguise himself. . . ."

"So you figured it was the right thing to do?" He

reaches into a pouch at his belt with one hand and points his wand at you with the other.

Desperate, you draw your sword and attack, slashing at the wizard's outstretched hand. He dodges you easily and then holds his other hand open. You see a bit of wet dirt there, along with a piece of a lime. He spits out a word you don't recognize, and the stuff in his hand vaporizes.

From that moment, you can't move. You're frozen so solid you can't even breathe. Just as everything goes black, you hear Halaster laugh.

"Welcome to life as a statue guarding the sanctuary. Hopefully, you can at least serve as a warning for the next fools."

THE END

You decide to let Spite test your suspicions for you. As he reaches into the desk drawer to pick up the spell book, you step out of the room, just in case.

"It's mine!" Spite says. "Halaster's precious spell book is finally all mine."

There's a loud *WHOOMPF* from inside the room that shakes the walls and knocks the door off one of its hinges. Despite being braced and ready, you still flinch at the noise.

After waiting for a full five seconds, you peer around the broken door and into the room. Spite is lying sprawled across the floor, the spell book in his right hand. Blood trickles from his nose and ears.

As carefully as you can, you creep into the room, still on the lookout for traps. If the past few minutes have taught you anything, it's that Halaster is incredibly protective of his valuables, and you don't want to wind up like Spite.

Despite checking the floor, walls, and ceiling for traps, you don't find anything suspicious. If you pick up the spell book, it might hurt you the way it did Spite, but in your experience, such spell traps have to be reset first.

It's probably safe to pick it up.

Turn to page 114 . . .

P lease!" you shout as you're yanked into the air once again. "You're my only hope!"

"Then you're out of luck," Halaster says. "This is the entrance to Halaster's sanctuary, and only the actual Halaster can enter it safely."

You boggle at that. "Isn't that you?"

As you slam into the floor once more, you blink, and Halaster becomes a humanoid fox-man.

"I'm afraid not. I'm an arcanaloth who works for Halaster. I impersonate him so I can run the school, but I'm not nearly as powerful as the real thing."

You want to weep in frustration and horror, but the metal monster takes that moment to kick you in the head. Knocked senseless, you can't see straight until you're hauled up toward the ceiling again.

"By the gods, no!" you say in a hoarse, beaten voice you barely recognize as your own. "How long will this go on?"

The fox-man gives you a sympathetic shrug. "Only as long as you're still breathing."

You hit the stone floor again and gasp in pain.

"From the look of you, that shouldn't be too much longer."

THE END

W ait!" you shout at Spite. "That spell book's mine!"

The boy turns on you, snarling in disbelief. "Are you insane? After all I've done to get here and grab this? After losing Dumara to that iron monster out there? I'm not going to let you betray me now!'

Your blade appears in your hand. "Speak so much as one word of a spell, and I'll cut out your tongue," you warn.

Spite scowls at you and lets an illusion that he's been holding up the entire time you've known him drop. This reveals him to be an old man with long white hair swept back from his wizened face.

"You think you can trifle with me, boy?" Spite — or whatever his real name might be — says. "I'm not just some child you can push around. I'm one of the greatest wizards of this age."

"Except Halaster," you say, finally understanding what the old man has done. "You actually disguised yourself as a child to sneak in here and steal your rival's spell book?"

The idea is so funny that you can't help but smile. The man had to pretend to be a boy to weasel his way into a school. That doesn't sound much like the work of a mighty wizard to you.

"There was no other way!" Spite thunders at you, irritated by your reaction. "And you're not going to stop me now that I'm so close."

No matter how hilarious you might find his protests, you're not going to let him get in your way. You circle around toward the desk, forcing Spite away from it by brandishing the tip of your sword at him. You take the book from him with your spare hand.

A magical rune flashes before your eyes as you raise the book to look at it. You don't have any time to react, but Spite spots it before you do and manages to throw himself to the floor.

Triggered by your action, the rune goes off, and there's a horrible *WHOOMPF* noise that blasts you flat onto your back. You can feel yourself going into shock, the life draining out of you as Spite pushes himself to his feet, chuckling the whole time.

"How perfect," he says, savoring the fact that he's the one laughing now. "Halaster's last trap takes out the one person who could have stopped me from stealing his spell book. And now it's mine!"

You try to stop him from taking the book from you, but you can't get your fingers to work. The last thing you hear is him cackling in triumph as he dashes from the room.

THE END

The images in this book were created by Allen Douglas, Andrew Mar, Bryan Syme, Chris Seaman, Christopher Moeller, Clint Cearley, Conceptopolis, Cynthia Sheppard, Cyril Van Der Haegen, David Palumbo, David Vargo, Emily Fiegenschuh, Eric Belisle, Ilya Shipkin, Jason Juta, Jim Pavelec, John Stanko, Kieran Yanner, Kurt Huggins and Zelda Devon, Michael Berube, Olga Drebas, Scott Murphy, Sidharth Chaturvedi, and Wayne England.

The cover illustrations were created by Cynthia Sheppard, Jesper Ejsing, and Titus Lunter.

CANDLEWICK
ENTERTAINMENT

Copyright © 2019 by Wizards of the Coast LLC
Written by Matt Forbeck
Designed by Wendy Bartlett
Edited by Kirsty Walters
Published in the U.K. 2019 by Studio Press Books,
part of Bonnier Books U.K.
All rights reserved.

First U.S. edition 2019
Library of Congress Catalog Card Number 2019938948
ISBN 978-1-5362-0924-2 (hardcover) 978-1-5362-0925-9 (paperback)
19 20 21 22 23 24 WKT 10 9 8 7 6 5 4 3 2 1
Printed in Shenzhen, Guangdong, China
Candlewick Press, 99 Dover Street, Somerville, Massachusetts 02144
visit us at www.candlewick.com

Don't miss the other Dungeons & Dragons®
Endless Quest® titles!

Escape the Underdark
Into the Jungle
To Catch a Thief
Big Trouble
Escape from Castle Ravenloft

Or these Dungeons & Dragons titles available from
Candlewick Press:

Monsters and Heroes of the Realms
Dungeonology